For

Gabriel

First published in Great Britain 2021 by Walker Books Ltd
87 Vauxhall Walk, London SE11 5HJ

2 4 6 8 10 9 7 5 3 1

© 2020 Lucy Cousins

The right of Lucy Cousins to be identified as author/illustrator of this work has been
asserted by her in accordance with the Copyright, Designs and Patents Act 1988.

This book has been typeset in Futura.
Handlettering by Lucy Cousins.

Printed in China

British Library Cataloguing in Publication Data:
a catalogue record for this book is available from the British Library.

ISBN 978-1-4063-8480-2

www.walker.co.uk

Let's Play MONSTERS!

Lucy Cousins

WALKER BOOKS
AND SUBSIDIARIES
LONDON • BOSTON • SYDNEY • AUCKLAND

My name is Gabriel
and I am three.
I like to play with monsters
but they can't catch me!

Come on, Josie,
I WANT TO PLAY!
You chase me
and I'll run away.

You be a monster
who is green and scary,
with sharp pointy teeth
and feet that are hairy.

MUNCH, CRUNCH, SCRUNCH, I'LL EAT YOU FOR MY LUNCH!

Hee, hee, hee!
But you can't
catch me!

Come on, Uncle Rufus,
I WANT TO PLAY!
You chase me
and I'll run away.

You be a monster
who's VERY VERY BIG,
with horns like a cow
and a tail like a pig.

OINK, OINK, MOO, I'M CHASING YOU!

Hee, hee, hee!
But you can't
catch me!

Come on, Kitty Cat,
I WANT TO PLAY!
You chase me
and I'll run away.

You be a monster
with long sharp claws,
all scritchy and scratchy
on your big yellow paws.

HISS, HISS, ROAR,
I'LL CHASE YOU OUT THE DOOR!

Hee, hee, hee!
But you can't
catch me!

Come on, Nonna,
I WANT TO PLAY!
You chase me
and I'll run away.

You be a monster
made of bright pink jelly
with big round eyes
and feet that are smelly.

SCHLOP, SCHLAP, SCHLUP, I'LL GOBBLE YOU UP!

Hee, hee, hee!
But you can't
catch me!

Come on, Flower,
I WANT TO PLAY!
You chase me
and I'll run away.

You be a monster
with a big yellow nose
and long green arms
and muddy brown toes.

FI, FO, FUM,
I'LL TICKLE YOUR TUM!

Hee, hee, hee!
But you can't
catch me!

Come on, Mummy,
I WANT TO PLAY!
You chase me
and I'll run away.

You be a monster
with spikes on your back
who eats little boys
with your teeth that are black.

GOBBLE, GOBBLE, GULP, I'LL EAT YOU UP!

Hee, hee, hee! But you can't catch me!

OH YES I CAN!

I'LL GOBBLE YOUR
TOES

AND I'LL NIBBLE YOUR
NOSE!

Now **YOU** be a monster with a funny green head, who is tired and sleepy and ready for bed.

Monster kisses,
one, two, three.

I love you
and you love me.